Are There BEARS in Starvation Lake?

by Gloria Whelan
illustrated by Lynne Cravath

For all my friends down the road
G.W.

To Sigi
L.C.

Library of Congress Cataloging-in-Publication Data
Whelan, Gloria.
Are there bears in Starvation Lake? / by Gloria Whelan ; illustrated by Lynne Cravath.
    p.   cm. — (Road to reading. Mile 5)
Summary: When Baylor and his fourth-grade class stay overnight at the Starvation Lake Ecology Center, he is nervous about what might happen, like getting lost or running into wild animals.
ISBN 0-307-26515-3 (pbk.) — ISBN 0-307-46515-2 (GB)
[1. Nature centers—Fiction. 2. School field trips—Fiction. 3. Animals—Fiction. 4. Interpersonal relations—Fiction.] I. Cravath, Lynne Woodcock, ill. II. Title. III. Series.

PZ7.W5718 Ar 2002
[Fic]—dc21
                                                            2001040861

 A GOLDEN BOOK • NEW YORK

ISBN: 0-307-26515-3 (pbk)
ISBN: 0-307-46515-2 (GB)

Printed in the United States of America

10   9   8   7   6   5   4   3   2   1

Contents

1. Cold Weather Can Kill You   1

2. Out into the Woods   8

3. Baylor's Gourmet Dinner   20

4. The Owl Call   26

5. Night Monsters   38

6. An Animal Attacks   45

7. Scat and Snow Fleas   51

8. Baylor Lost   59

9. Something Warm, Something
   Furry   64

1
Cold Weather Can Kill You

It was another perfectly awful day in Starvation Lake. The school bus slid to a stop on the icy road. Baylor Proust could just make out a snow-covered sign swinging in the wind. It said Starvation Lake Ecology Center.

The center was on the far shore of Starvation Lake. Baylor had driven by it with his parents, but that had been in the summer. Now everything was covered with snow.

Starvation Lake Elementary School's fourth-grade students sprang out of their seats, eager for their overnight at the

1

center. They had worked hard to raise money for the overnight. Now the day they had looked forward to was here.

The bus door opened with a whoosh and a squeak. As the other kids pushed their way out, Baylor hunkered down in his seat. He wished he were invisible. He wished he were a million miles away.

This afternoon the worst thing in the world had happened. When Baylor got on the bus, his mother had *cried* because he was going away for the night. Tears had actually run down her cheeks. The whole fourth grade had seen her.

What if the kids teased him about it? Baylor was so embarrassed. He longed to stay on the bus, but Elvera, the bus driver, called out, "Okay, Baylor, I'm not taking you home with me. You're out of here."

Baylor blundered down the aisle. With his sweaters and down jacket and his special pillow, he had trouble squeezing out the door. Elvera gave him a gentle push.

"Watch out for bears!" Elvera called.

"Are there bears in Starvation Lake?" Dawn Zonder whispered to Theresa Bloncheck.

"Sure," Theresa said. "They're all over Desolation County. One time someone brought a bear cub to my mom, thinking it was a puppy." Theresa's mom was the animal rescue officer.

Dawn shivered. Baylor shivered, too. *Bears?* He turned back toward the bus, but it had already pulled away.

Next to him, Bethany Conway was looking at the tall pines blanketed with snow. Baylor heard her sigh. Bethany loved to write poems about nature. Nature was everywhere here.

"It's so beautiful," Bethany said to Theresa. "I wonder if there are any dead animals around." Bethany's poems were usually sad.

"We'll all be dead if we bump into bears," said Stacey Ward.

Tommy Kewaysaw shook his head. "I've never heard of the bears around here eating people."

"That's because the people they eat can't tell anyone about it," Theresa said.

A man greeted them. He was tall and sturdy like one of the pine trees. His windburned face had the beginnings of a black beard. Theresa and Stacey looked at each other. Baylor could tell they thought the man was handsome. "Welcome to the

Starvation Lake Ecology Center," he said. "I'm Nicholas Neddle, the naturalist from the center. Just call me Nick."

"It's the whole catalog," Marvin Mallow whispered to Mark Ellenberger. It was true. Nick had on L.L.Bean Snowclaw boots and a Bean Rugged Ridge parka. His Bean Duofold underwear was visible under his shirt collar.

"You can drop your stuff at the boys' and girls' dorms. Then meet me at the lodge." Nick pointed to a large log cabin.

A few minutes later, Marvin, Kevin Brown, Mark, and Tommy were gathered around the fireplace in the lodge, warming up. Baylor stood off by himself. The smoke from the fire made him cough.

"Wow!" Marvin said. "The fireplace is almost as big as our living room."

"Look at that neat stuffed hawk and the stuffed beaver on the mantel," Mark said.

"I don't think an ecology center ought to kill animals just to stuff them," Kevin said. "There's probably a law against that." Both of Kevin's parents were lawyers.

Nick overheard Kevin. "We don't kill them," he explained. "They either die a natural death or get hit by a car. People bring them to us after they're dead."

"That's just like your place," Tommy said to Mark. Mark's father owned a funeral home.

"Sometimes we don't stuff them," Nick said. "We cook them. I've had a lot of meals from roadkill. Quite a few squirrels in the spring and fall. You'd be surprised how tasty they are. Raccoons aren't bad either, but wild turkeys are the best."

"Marvin's family has a turkey farm," Tommy said.

"Well, *those* birds are raised to be eaten," Nick said. "The turkeys around here are safe as long as they stay near the center and don't get hit by a car."

Baylor sighed. He remembered seeing the turkeys on the Mallow farm lined up by the barn during Thanksgiving week. They were waiting to be zapped, plucked, and boxed. Baylor imagined bringing the turkeys here where they wouldn't be harmed. He saw himself shepherding them along the highway.

Nick interrupted Baylor's daydream. "Okay, kids, we're going to talk about how cold weather can kill you."

Baylor nearly fainted.

2
Out into the Woods

"I want you all to bundle up," Nick said. "We're going to have some fun. We're going out into the woods to learn how to keep from freezing to death. And how to not get lost in the woods."

Fun? Baylor couldn't believe they were actually going out in the cold and wind so they could wander around the woods, freezing and losing themselves.

"We're going to use the buddy system here," Nick said. "Each one of you will be responsible for making sure your partner is all right."

Bethany and Dawn, and Theresa and

Stacey paired off. Mark chose Kevin. Tommy and Marvin were partners. Baylor wasn't surprised that no one had picked him.

When Nick saw Baylor standing alone, he said to Kevin and Mark, "Baylor can be part of your group." Kevin groaned.

Baylor pretended not to notice. "How will we get around in two feet of snow?" he asked.

"No problem. We've got snowshoes for everyone," Nick said.

There was a big cheer. Nick opened a cupboard and began passing out snow-shoes. He showed them how to strap the snowshoes on their feet and how to lift one foot over the other.

As soon as the kids tried to turn around in their snowshoes, they fell down. They seemed to think falling in snowshoes was fun. Baylor felt a headache coming on.

Theresa said, "I feel like a little dog with big paws."

Only Tommy was walking confidently along. "Before he worked at the casino," Tommy said, "my dad used to go trapping in the winter with my grandpa. They'd take me along."

As they trooped outdoors, Nick said, "Here's the mantra for your visit—*stay together*. I want you all to repeat it."

"Stay together," the class chanted.

"Now that we're outside," Nick went on, "you should be aware of hypothermia. Can anyone tell me what that means?"

Every hand went up. Ms. LaForest, the class's fourth-grade teacher, had prepared them for the overnight.

Bethany said, "*Hypo* in front of a word means 'not enough.' *Therm* is a measurement of heat. *Hypothermia* means you don't have enough heat."

"Very good," Nick said. He looked a little disappointed not to break the news. "There are five stages of hypothermia. In the first, you can't stop shivering. In the second stage, you have trouble speaking. In the third, you don't know what you're doing. In the fourth, you lose consciousness. In the fifth, you're dead."

Immediately the kids began to shiver, slur their speech, and say crazy things. Mark fell on the snow, shut his eyes, and pretended he was dead. Baylor figured Mark had seen lots of people like that.

"Okay, kids." Nick's voice became ultraserious. "This is no laughing matter."

Everyone quieted down. Baylor had never felt so cold. He zipped up his parka and pulled the flaps down over his ears. When he realized he couldn't hear Nick, he pulled them up again.

Nick said, "Another thing to worry about is getting lost. I want you to learn how to use a compass. Someday you might be in the woods where there aren't any roads or trails. You could turn the wrong way and be lost before you know it."

"This guy is a laugh a minute," Marvin whispered to Tommy.

Nick handed each student a compass. "The red arrow always points north," he explained. He looked pleased, as if the way the arrow pointed were his idea.

Kevin turned around a couple of times, trying to confuse the compass. But the arrow kept pointing north. "How does it know?" Kevin asked Nick.

"It points to a magnetic pole. Not the North Pole, the *magnetic* pole." All the kids nodded as if they understood.

"Now, suppose you want to go east," Nick said. He showed them how to turn a part of the compass and watch a different arrow, all the while remembering that the red arrow pointed north. They took turns going in different directions.

"Okay, kids, here's a map, and you're on your own. If you follow the map, it will lead you to the lodge. I'll see you there. Don't forget the mantra—*stay together*." Nick handed Baylor the map and a sheet of directions. Then he made a big point of striding away.

Baylor was plenty nervous. He didn't

like being in charge of the map. What if he led the class the wrong way? Baylor looked at the directions. He read out, "Go north to the cedar swamp."

"That's easy," Stacey said. "We just go in the direction of the red arrow."

They walked along behind Baylor. Baylor was amazed that everyone was following him. In a short time they reached the swamp. There were heart-shaped tracks all over the snow.

Tommy said, "Those are deer tracks. Deer winter in the swamp. They can browse the cedar and hemlock trees. It's warm here because the trees shelter the deer from the wind."

They peered into the dark swamp. It had a damp, ugly smell. The snow was piled up over dead cedar logs. Here and there where the snow was thin, Baylor could see brown muck. He shivered.

"I'll bet you could sink right down into the mud," Mark said. He poked his snowshoe into the swamp. It got stuck. Tommy and Marvin had to pull him out. Big clumps of mud clung to the snowshoe.

While Baylor waited for Mark to clean off his snowshoe, he thought he saw something moving in the trees. Maybe it was a bear. The map trembled in his hand.

"Let's get going," Tommy said. "What's next, Baylor?"

Baylor looked at the directions. "It says to go east toward a group of pine trees."

"What if we get lost and they never find us?" Dawn asked.

"We won't get lost," Tommy said. "I saw Nick sneaking around behind the trees, watching us. He was having a fit when Mark stuck his foot in the swamp."

Baylor breathed a sigh of relief. So that was what he had seen. Everyone felt safer—and only a little irritated that Nick wouldn't leave them on their own.

"Let's show him we know he's there," Theresa said.

They went to work building a snowman that looked like Nick. They used twigs to make his beard, and pinecones to give him huge eyes that stuck way out. Kevin took off his L.L.Bean Super 200 watch cap and put it on the snowman. The kids were careful not to look at the trees where Nick was hiding.

Giggling, they clustered around Baylor and the map again.

Mark peered over Baylor's shoulder.

"Now the directions say to head south to the lodge," Mark said. "That's easy. We just go in the opposite direction of the red arrow."

When they reached the lodge, Nick was waiting for them. He tried to look surprised that they had found their way back. He didn't mention the snowman, but Kevin found his cap on one of the chairs.

Nick called, "Okay, kids, time to warm up. We're off to the recreation building for a game of dodgeball. I'll join you and play on whichever side needs me." Baylor saw a fierce gleam in Nick's eyes.

Dawn was quick to say, "I think I have a headache. I better lie down for a while." She hurried away to the dormitory. Baylor knew Dawn hated having the ball come speeding right at her.

Actually Baylor hated dodgeball, too. He thought about saying he didn't feel well, even though it wasn't true. For once he felt pretty good.

"Come on, Baylor," Nick said. "You can be on my team."

The ball whizzed back and forth. Sometimes Baylor got out of the way, and sometimes he didn't. But even if the ball hit him, it didn't knock him down or kill him, and it hardly even hurt. If only the ball had been softer, it would have been almost fun.

3
Baylor's Gourmet Dinner

The game of dodgeball made everyone pretty hungry. Bethany brought Dawn back to the lodge from the dormitory. The class settled at the long tables in the lodge's dining room.

Nick passed out cartons of milk. Each student had brought dinner in a lunch box or paper bag. At school Baylor usually sat by himself, but now Mark and Kevin were sitting right across from him. He wondered if they'd make fun of him when they saw what his mother had packed.

With a sigh, Baylor opened his lunch box. He took out carrot sticks, celery sticks, broccoli and cauliflower florets, slices of zucchini, and a yogurt dip. A chunk of tofu was carefully wrapped in foil. For dessert, there were dried figs and apricots. As a special treat, his mother had packed her wheat-germ cookies. The cookies *looked* good, but Baylor always had trouble biting through them.

The noisy table suddenly quieted down. All the kids were staring at Baylor's dinner. Their faces had pitying looks, as if Baylor were starving to death right in front of them. Baylor wished he could climb into his lunch box.

Now they'll laugh at me, thought Baylor. *They'll move away, and in a couple of minutes, I'll be all by myself like I usually am.*

Instead Marvin said, "Hey, Baylor,

want to trade some broccoli for part of a turkey burrito with salsa on the side?"

"I'll eat your zucchini and cauliflower for you," Theresa said. She pushed a hot dog roll and a thermos toward Baylor. A string was hanging out of the thermos. Baylor pulled the string, and a nice warm hot dog popped out.

"How about some of my fried bread?" Tommy asked. He reached over for Baylor's tofu. When it slid out of his hand, he didn't bother to pick it up.

Stacey took a dried fig and gave Baylor half of one of Weird Mom's anchovy-and-sardine wraps.

Mark handed Baylor a Twinkie and picked up a wheat-germ cookie. Bethany took the other cookie and gave Baylor a square of chocolate pudding cake that was

left over from the church supper.

Baylor ate every crumb, a blissful look on his face. In all his life he had never had a hot dog ("They grind up cows' udders, dear," his mom had said) or a Twinkie ("I'm sure the vanilla cream would be too rich for you, dear"). Even the anchovy-and-sardine wrap tasted better than cauliflower dipped in yogurt. It was the best meal Baylor had ever had.

As soon as the tables were cleared, Nick announced, "We're going to take an owl walk. Put on your snowshoes and bundle up—hats, mittens, boots, the works."

Since Baylor had more to put on than anyone else, it took him a little longer. He thought about leaving off one of his sweaters, or maybe the long scarf that choked him. But suppose he got chilled and caught a cold and got pneumonia?

It was dark outside. The only light came from a full moon. It made the snow silver and cast long, striped shadows from the pine trees. Because the moon was so bright, only a few stars were visible.

"Who can find the Big Dipper?" Nick asked.

Tommy pointed it out. "It looks like a saucepan with a long handle."

"Very good," Nick said. "Okay, now I want everyone to draw a line in your mind between the two stars at the farthest end of the saucepan. See the star they point to? That's the North Star. If you get lost in the woods, that will tell you which direction you're going."

At the words "lost in the woods," Baylor inched closer to the other kids.

4
The Owl Call

Nick led the kids into the woods. They all stayed together. Baylor kept Mark on one side of him and Kevin on the other. Their shadows moved with them across the snow.

"I didn't know that you could see your shadow without the sun," Stacey said. "It's totally weird."

"*Shhh*, everyone," Nick said. He had an excited look on his face. "I want you to listen hard." Suddenly he made a strange sound. It wasn't exactly a screech or a scream or a shout. He seemed to be saying, "Who-cooks-for-you-all." It was eerie.

Everyone was quiet. Nick called again, "Who-cooks-for-you-all."

From a distance, there was a faint answer. Something was calling back, "Who-cooks-for-you-all."

"What is it?" Baylor whispered.

"It's an owl," Tommy said.

"It's a barred owl," Nick said.

"Why does it say that?" Baylor asked.

Nick shrugged. "That's just what it says," Nick told him, "like you say 'hello' or 'good morning.' "

Baylor thought "hello" or "good morning" made a lot more sense than "who-cooks-for-you-all," but he didn't want to hurt Nick's feelings.

"Who wants to try calling the owl?" Nick asked.

They each took a turn. Sometimes the

owl called back. Sometimes it didn't. At last it was silent.

"Must have moved on," Nick said. "Okay, we'll try something else." He reached into one of about a dozen pockets in his parka and pulled out a tape recorder. "Owls aren't the only ones out here tonight," he said.

Baylor looked nervously around. There seemed to be more shadows than there had been a couple of minutes before. Dawn reached for Bethany's sleeve.

Nick informed them, "The next thing you'll hear is the cry of a wounded rabbit."

"Oh!" Dawn said. "Let's rescue it and make it better."

"It's not a *real* wounded rabbit," Nick said. "That is, it's real, but it's not actually here."

Everyone stared at him. He held up the tape recorder. "Someone taped the cry of a wounded rabbit."

"Why?" Baylor asked.

"So you can learn about predators," Nick said. "Right now in these woods, there are owls and coyotes and foxes that would like to eat a wounded rabbit for supper."

"Gross," Theresa said.

"It's just the food chain," Nick said. "Everything eats something else. If you were in Africa, a hungry lion might eat *you*."

Nick turned on the tape recorder. They heard a horrific scream.

Baylor jumped right up in the air. Dawn put her hands over her ears. There was complete silence as everyone waited for a real predator to come and eat the imaginary wounded rabbit.

Baylor worried about what kinds of predators might appear. Elvera had mentioned bears. And what about wolves? If only he had eaten the vegetables and tofu his mother had given him, instead of all those delicious things! Probably with a hot dog and a Twinkie inside him, he would taste better to a wolf.

A shadow glided across the snow. Overhead they saw a large bird silhouetted against the moon. While they all held their breath, the bird circled twice and flew off.

Nick seemed surprised. "Gee," he said, "that was a great horned owl. First one I've seen this year."

Another shadow moved among the

trees. Marvin sneezed. Something scurried off.

Everyone looked at Marvin. "I couldn't help it," he said. "There must have been a turkey feather in my mitten. It got up my nose."

"I think that was a coyote attracted by the cry of the rabbit," Nick said. "He won't be back tonight. What do you say we have some hot cocoa in front of the fireplace and then turn in?"

Back at the lodge, Baylor was happy to peel off his sweaters and parka and scarf. He sat down in front of the fireplace to warm up. He had hoped Kevin and Mark would sit next to him, but they wandered over to the other boys.

"Let's sing a few songs," Nick suggested. "Does your school have its own song?"

In a very sweet voice, Dawn sang the Starvation Lake Elementary School song:

Starvation Lake, we're for you,
We're here for you to cheer for you,
We have no fear for you, Starvation Lake.
Rah! Rah! Rah!

Everyone joined in on the *rah rahs*. They sang "Take Me Out to the Ball Game" and "She'll Be Comin' Round the Mountain." Kevin started to sing the Putrid Armpits' new hit. The Putrid Armpits was their favorite band. They all knew the words. "If I were an octopus," they sang, "I'd give you a hundred hugs."

Nick jumped up. "Okay, kids, time to turn in. See you in the morning."

As they made their way back to the

dormitory, Baylor heard Marvin whisper to Kevin, "I've got an idea that'll give the girls the scare of their lives. You with me?"

Kevin nodded.

"How about you?" Marvin looked at Baylor.

Baylor decided that anything that would be scary for the girls would probably scare him, too. He wanted to say he wasn't interested, but then he remembered they had shared their dinner with him.

"Sure," he said.

After the boys were settled in the dorm, Marvin told them his plan. Baylor didn't like the sound of it. He cleared his throat. "Uh, I don't think we're supposed to go outside," he said.

"Nick didn't actually *say* we couldn't, did he?" Kevin asked.

"Well, he sort of implied it." Baylor was thinking of how cold and dark it would be outside. Of course, he didn't want to admit that. They would think he was afraid. And he was.

"Come on, Baylor." Mark tossed Baylor his jacket. Tommy, Kevin, and Marvin were already heading for the door. Baylor pulled on his extra sweater. He tied his scarf around his neck and struggled into his parka. He put on his cap and mittens. It took a long time. He was hoping the boys would get tired of waiting and leave. Instead they watched impatiently, urging him to hurry.

All Baylor's things were cold and damp from the melting snow. He followed the boys out of the dorm. In the pale moon-light, the pine trees appeared to stretch right up to the sky. Their branches reached toward Baylor like monstrous arms. He wished he were back inside.

They had taken only a few steps when the shadow of an animal darted across their path. "Looked like a big cat," Kevin said.

"Maybe a raccoon," Mark suggested.

"No, it was black," Baylor said. "It went right by me, and it smelled kind of funny." Baylor stood looking in the direction the animal had taken.

"Hey, Baylor," Tommy whispered, "you're falling behind. Remember what Nick said—*stay together.*"

Baylor didn't see why they had to do what Nick said when they were doing something Nick wouldn't approve of to begin with. He trudged after the other boys. He didn't want to end up all alone in the woods.

The five boys made five creeping shadows on the snow as they slouched toward the girls' dormitory. It was so cold that the snow squeaked beneath their boots. *Would they notice if I turned back?* Baylor wondered.

Kevin tugged at his parka. "Hurry up, Baylor."

Baylor moved a little faster, but he had a feeling something bad was going to happen—and that he would be there when it did.

5
Night Monsters

In their dormitory, the girls were getting ready for bed. It was the first time they had all spent the night together. Stacey said, "It's just like being in college." She passed around her green nail polish for everyone to try.

"Isn't green kind of a strange color?" Theresa asked.

"It's no stranger than red," Stacey said.

Bethany asked, "Did you see what Baylor's mom packed for his dinner? I felt so sorry for him."

"It must be hard to have a mom who worries so much about you," Stacey said.

Suddenly the girls stopped talking. They had just remembered something. Dawn was fluffing up her stuffed moose.

"How is your mom doing?" Theresa asked Dawn. Dawn's mother was in a hospital downstate waiting for a new heart. Dawn had come to Starvation Lake to live with her grandmother while her dad stayed near the hospital.

Dawn looked at them, her eyes very wide open. In a small voice, she said, "Dad thinks Mom will probably get her heart next week." All the girls were silent for a minute. Having a new heart put into you was something to think about.

"Will you go downstate?" Stacey asked.

Dawn sighed a great sigh. "Yes," she said, "afterward." Dawn looked as if she might be ready to cry.

To cheer her up, Theresa said, "I wrote a new chapter in my novel, *California Sunshine*. Would you like to hear it?" Theresa wrote a chapter nearly every day.

Dawn nodded. All the girls gathered around Theresa.

"Well," Theresa said, "I got the idea from the ecology center. Here goes. . . ."

Amber and her friends were spending the day at an ecology center in the middle of the California woods. It was another beautiful, warm, sunny day. Amber was wearing a safari suit and a hat with a wide brim that turned up on one side. There were many tame wild animals, like bears and tigers, in the woods. The animals sat up and rolled over when you asked them to. There was a stream with alligators, but

California alligators don't bother you. Amber and her friends picked pepperoni off the pepperoni trees and cooked a pizza over a campfire for their lunch. Then they went to have dinner with Leonardo DiCaprio.

Stacey said, "I don't think there are alligators in California. I don't think you can say 'tame wild animals.' Ms. LaForest would say that's a contradiction."

"That's for something you're handing in," Theresa said. "This is fiction. You're supposed to use your imagination."

Bethany nodded in agreement. She had just finished a poem. She cleared her throat, and everyone knew she was going to read it to them. In her usual cheerful voice, she recited:

The Owl

In the moon's silver light
The rabbit hops over the snow.
In the silent night
The owl swoops low.
Now he will seek
With a sharp, cruel beak
To satisfy his appetite.

Just as the girls were thinking about the "sharp, cruel beak," something brushed against the dorm. It sounded as if a large animal was nearby. The girls looked at each other. There was a loud bump and the sound of claws scratching at the window. A second later, there was a wild cry.

Dawn grabbed her moose, climbed into bed, and pulled the covers over her head. Bethany remembered she hadn't said her good-night prayers. Theresa and Stacey just looked at each other.

"Turn out the lights," Theresa whispered. Stacey reached for the switch.

"If you turn off the lights, it will be dark," Dawn said in a shaky, muffled voice.

"There's nothing to be afraid of. It's not an animal," Stacey said. She turned off the switch. "Come and look." She was standing on her bed, peering out the window. The other girls gathered around her.

In the light of the moon, they could see several shadowy figures hunkered down next to their cabin. There was another bloodcurdling scream. It came from one of the figures . . . one of the five fourth-grade boys standing under the window.

6
An Animal Attacks

Marvin scraped a tree branch across the side of the girls' dormitory. Then he held the branch up and dragged it against a window. It made a satisfying clawlike sound. Mark whacked the side of the building with a piece of wood while Tommy gave a bloodcurdling scream.

Baylor shuddered. He crept close to the other boys so that he wouldn't be off by himself.

Suddenly the lights inside the dorm went out. "Wow!" Marvin said. "They must really be scared."

Baylor couldn't help thinking of Dawn.

She was usually scared anyhow. He wasn't so sure it was a good idea to scare her even more.

They crouched under the window. "Tommy," Marvin whispered, "scream again."

Tommy screamed.

The window opened and a pitcher of water flooded over them. Tommy screamed for real.

"Hey!" Kevin shouted. "That's cold!" The water ran over Baylor's cap and onto his parka. Marvin was shaking like a wet dog. The girls leaned out of the window, laughing. Even Dawn's moose was hanging out of the window.

"The water is starting to freeze!" Baylor wailed. He felt as if he were turning into an icicle.

The boys fell all over themselves in their hurry to get back inside. They had almost reached the dormitory when Baylor spotted the black animal they had seen earlier. Before he could say anything, they were right on it. The animal just stood there. Baylor noticed a white streak on the animal's back. So did everyone else. But it was too late.

"Ugh! Oh! It stinks!" Everyone was crying out. The skunk scurried away, but the horrible smell was everywhere.

A flashlight shone on them. "What's all the racket?" Nick called. He ran toward them. "Why are you guys outside?" He stopped suddenly. "Oh, no! Okay, follow me. Just don't get too close."

When they reached the dorm, Nick held out a large plastic trash bag. "Put your outdoor clothes in here. I'll toss them in the washing machine. Then nice warm showers for everyone. But first I'll get the tomato juice. You'll need to use it before you shower." Nick hurried away.

The boys looked at each other. *Tomato juice?* They weren't thirsty. Baylor didn't even like tomato juice.

When Nick came back, he had several restaurant-sized cans of tomato juice. "Here's the drill, fellows. Rub the tomato juice all over you—in your hair, too. Some people say it gets rid of the smell. I'm not sure . . . but we've got to try something. Hope you don't mind if I open the window a little, and I'll just see to washing and drying your clothes. I can't say I want to hang around in here any longer than I have to."

He stopped at the doorway. "I guess I don't have to tell you that it was pretty stupid to go outdoors after hours." He gave them a long look. "No, I guess I don't. See you later."

The boys took turns pouring tomato juice over their heads and standing in the shower. Baylor used a lot of soap, and at least he smelled better. But when he got out of the shower, his hair was bright pink.

7
Scat and Snow Fleas

At breakfast, Nick said, "Sorry, kids, all we've got this morning is orange juice. The tomato juice seems to be gone."

Theresa had a big smile on her face. "I wonder what happened to it," she said.

Stacey grinned. "I like your hair, Baylor."

Dawn asked in a very soft voice, "Did you boys hear anything last night? We thought there might be an animal prowling around."

"It looked like a skunk." Bethany moved away from the boys' table. "Maybe we should open the window a little bit."

"No need for that," Nick said. "We're going outside soon. Before you leave today, we'll be spending some time in the woods."

When they got outdoors, Nick told them, "Here's what we're going to do. You'll keep your buddy system, but there will be two teams. The boys will be one team and the girls the other. Let's see which team does the best job of finding out how animals get by in winter. We'll try to discover what they eat, where they live, and how they survive in the cold."

He started to ask if they knew what *hibernation* meant, but before he finished the question, everyone's hand went up.

"It's when animals sort of hole up and go to sleep, or partly to sleep, so they can keep warm and not have to eat too much."

Baylor took a long breath—that was a lot to get out.

"Is there anything you kids don't know?" Nick said. "Okay, keep an eye out for animal and bird tracks, dens where animals hibernate, and scat. I suppose you know what scat is."

The whole class looked blank. The truth was Ms. LaForest hadn't known just how to explain it. So she never had.

"It's animal poop," Nick told them. "Every animal's scat is different."

"Oh, gross," Theresa said.

As Nick handed out guides with pictures of different kinds of animal tracks, scat, and burrows, snowballs began flying. Baylor dodged the snowballs. Soon, with all his outdoor clothes on, he was feeling hot and thirsty. He scooped up a handful of cold snow and stuffed it in his mouth.

"You sure you want to eat those fleas?" Nick called to Baylor.

Baylor stared at him.

"Take a look, everyone," Nick said.

The class crowded around Baylor. Nick had a magnifying glass. But even without it, they could see black dots hopping around on top of the snow.

"Those are snow fleas," Nick said. "You don't see them in summer, because they live underground. They eat the mold and fungus on old leaves." He put his hand near the snow. Soon it was covered with the tiny fleas. When he moved his hand, they sprang back onto the snow.

Baylor thought he was going to be sick. What if his mother found out he had swallowed fleas? And not just any fleas, but fleas that eat mold and fungus. His stomach started to churn.

Marvin pounded Baylor on the back. "Fleas are nothing," Marvin said. "We have them all the time because of the turkeys."

"Okay, off you go," Nick said. "And remember the mantra—*stay together*. I'll blow my whistle in half an hour and I want you all back here with notes and drawings about what you've seen. I'll decide which team found the most interesting evidence of how animals get through the winter."

The kids wandered off in different directions. Still spitting out snow, Baylor trailed along behind Kevin and Mark.

"Let's get away from the rest of the class," Mark said. "The deeper we go into the woods, the more stuff we'll find."

Baylor wanted to object, but he knew

they wouldn't listen to him. Mark and Kevin lifted one snowshoe over the other and hurried off. Baylor galumphed after them.

"Come on, Baylor," Mark called. "You're taking forever."

A light snow started falling. At first the flakes were no more than a movement in the air. Soon they grew larger. Baylor's glasses were covered with snow.

"Hey, look at this," Mark said. There were tracks in the snow. He consulted the track guide. "Must be a rabbit," he announced.

Baylor wiped the snow from his glasses and studied the guide. "It's a jackrabbit," he corrected.

"Whatever. I'll draw a picture of the tracks," Kevin said.

"Look, Kevin," Mark called. "Scat."

"That's revolting," Baylor said. He squinched his eyes shut while Kevin and Mark pored over the scat guide.

"Deer scat," Mark said.

Baylor sighed. What would his mother think if she saw him out in the snow studying animal poop? When he opened his eyes again, Mark and Kevin were out of sight. Baylor followed their tracks, but the snow was coming down hard. Soon their footprints were covered over.

Baylor found himself getting deeper and deeper into the woods. He called out, but there was no answer. A panicky feeling crept over him.

Either he had lost Kevin and Mark, or Kevin and Mark had lost him.

8
Baylor Lost

As soon as they heard Nick's whistle, everyone hurried back, eager to show off what they had seen. Tommy and Marvin had found squirrel tracks and wild turkey tracks.

"I recognized the turkey tracks right away," Marvin said. "And we found porcupine scat."

"We saw a place where a deer had been lying down," Tommy told Nick. "The snow was all pressed down in a sort of circle. There was deer scat nearby."

Mark and Kevin showed their pictures. Mark said, "I've been in the woods a lot, but I guess before this, I never really looked at what I was seeing. There's lots of stuff out there if you search for it."

"We found a tree stump where a squirrel sat eating a pinecone," Tommy said. "Pinecone scales were scattered over the snow."

After the boys had finished, the girls had a turn. Theresa said, "We saw beaver tracks. You could see where the beaver's tail had dragged through the snow."

Stacey chimed in, "We found an otter's tracks and a slide the otters had made on the bank of the lake."

Bethany said, "I found a folded leaf, and inside the leaf was a sort of cocoon where something was sleeping. And look at what Dawn found."

Dawn had made a drawing of a patch

of snow covered with tiny tracks and tracks from a large bird. She said in a horrified voice, "There were some drops of *blood*."

"It was real blood," Bethany said with a pleased smile. She had already started to make up another poem.

Looking very impressed, Nick studied the drawing. "My guess is an owl swooped down on a vole and ate it."

"What's a vole?" Kevin asked.

"It's a little like a mouse. You can see where the owl's wings swept away the snow. It looks like the girls are going to win this one."

Kevin said, "We probably could have found more stuff if we didn't have to wait for Baylor all the time." Kevin looked around. Mark looked around. They had

startled looks on their faces. At the same time, they both said, "Where's Baylor?"

Nick stared at them. "What do you mean, 'Where's Baylor?' He's your buddy. You're supposed to know where he is."

Mark and Kevin felt awful. "I guess we lost him," Mark said.

"You lost Baylor?" said Dawn in a small, shocked voice.

Kevin had a worried look on his face. "If anything happens to him," Kevin said, "it's our responsibility. His mother could sue us."

"Never mind the lawsuits," Nick said. "Let's just concentrate on finding Baylor. I want you to lead us to the last spot where you remember seeing him. And let's hurry. The snow is coming down fast."

9
Something Warm, Something Furry

About the time the kids discovered he was missing, Baylor was struggling through the woods. Nothing seemed familiar. In the heavy snow, everything looked like a big white bump or a small white bump or just some flat white stuff.

"Hello?" he shouted. "Is anyone out here?" His voice vanished in the wind. He had never felt so alone in his life.

Baylor thought about Nick's lecture on hypothermia. He was certainly shivering, his voice was a little shaky, and he wasn't sure what he was doing. But he was still conscious and he wasn't dead—yet.

Baylor spotted a couple of huge old trees that had fallen on top of each other. The dirt was scooped out under the logs, making a shelter. *I'll scooch into the opening until someone finds me,* he thought. *If anyone ever does.*

On his way to the shelter, a branch from a fir tree snapped back, knocking off his glasses. He groped around in the snow until he found them. It would be awful if he lost them. He decided to keep them in his pocket. He could still see the fallen trees ahead, but they were blurry.

As he got closer, he noticed something strange. Steam was coming from a hole in the snow over the fallen logs. It might be fog or mist, but why was it only over those logs?

Still, the steam cheered him a little.

Maybe it was warm in the shelter under the logs. Anxious to get out of the snow, he bent down to squeeze into the hollow.

Then Baylor noticed that dried leaves were scattered around the entrance to the dugout. He reached into the opening to check how big the space was. He felt something. It was warm. It was furry. It moved. It gave a sleepy grunt.

He sprang up, too terrified to run.

"Baylor!" someone called. The voices were coming closer.

"There he is!" another person shouted.

Nick came running toward him.

"What do you mean going off by yourself? Didn't you remember the mantra, *stay*—" Nick stopped mid-mantra. He looked closely at the pile of logs behind Baylor. Then he slapped his head. "Wow!

Look what Baylor found! We've all been wondering where that old black bear was hiding out this winter. Fantastic! His den was right here and we didn't even know it. Baylor, you're a genius."

Nick pointed out the den with its bed of dried leaves and the breathing hole where the steam came out.

"Won't the bear attack us?" Dawn whispered.

"No. He's hibernating, so he's ninety percent asleep. But let's leave him alone. Come on, kids, we'll go back to the lodge and give the bear some space."

They stood and watched the den a minute longer before turning around.

Nick said, "Well, Baylor's find trumps the owl and the vole. I guess this time the boys win."

A big shout went up from the boys. They crowded around Baylor and thumped him on the back.

The girls didn't feel too bad. They could win a contest anytime, but how often could they stand next to a snoozing bear in his den?

Only Kevin and Mark were a little disappointed. "If we'd stayed with Baylor, we would have found the bear, too," Kevin said. "I'm not letting him out of my sight."

"Weren't you scared?" Stacey asked Baylor.

Baylor didn't say a word. Even though they were far from the bear's den, he was still too terrified to get any words out.

Everyone thought he was quiet because he was so modest. That impressed them even more. Not only was he a hero, but he was too cool to talk about it. If one of them had been up in a helicopter looking down, it would have been easy to tell where Baylor was—right in the middle with everyone gathered around him.

At the top of a hill, Kevin called out, "Hey, look, there's Starvation Lake."

They all looked solemnly out across the frozen circle toward the town of Starvation Lake.

"The school seems really far away," Marvin said.

"Wait until we tell Ms. LaForest how we used snowshoes," Kevin said.

"And what happened with the skunk," Theresa added with a wicked smile.

"And how Baylor found a bear," Dawn said softly.

Tommy high-fived Baylor.

"Let's keep moving," Nick said. "The school bus will be waiting for you."

When he heard the words "school bus," Baylor blushed. Would the kids remember how his mother had cried when he'd left for the overnight?

Bethany noticed Baylor's red face. She guessed what he was thinking. "Don't worry about your mom crying. That's how mothers are, Baylor," she said. "My mom cried the first time I spent a night away with the kids' choir at church."

"My mom cried, too," Kevin added, "when I went to the Junior Lawyers of America meeting."

Baylor felt better. He looked around. A hawk rose from a tree branch and glided across the sky. Three blue jays, sounding like a creaky gate, called out. A black

About the Author

Since she lives in northern Michigan, Gloria Whelan always keeps an eye out for wild animals when she goes outside. "I go blackberry picking in August," she says. "And the bears pick where I pick. I've seen plenty of paw prints. But unlike Baylor, I've never actually seen a bear!"

The winner of the 2000 National Book Award for Young People's Literature, Gloria Whelan is known for writing well-crafted historical fiction. Her books include *Homeless Bird, The Wanigan,* and the two previous books about the kids of Starvation Lake Elementary School, *Welcome to Starvation Lake* and *Rich and Famous in Starvation Lake.*

squirrel darted out in front of Baylor and scampered up a pine.

Dawn tapped Baylor on the shoulder. "Look," she said. She pointed out a hare. Its fur was a white winter coat. Baylor could hardly see it against the snow. He turned and smiled at Dawn.

From the moment the overnight had started, there had been something for Baylor to worry about and something to be afraid of. For the first time, he was just enjoying himself.

Baylor walked along with the other kids. Snow from the tree branches over-head sifted silently down on him. He had touched a bear. He had played dodgeball. He had washed his hair with tomato juice and eaten a hot dog and a Twinkie.

He had never been so happy.